The Last Days
of Fraggle Rock

By Louise Gikow
Pictures by Sue Venning

Muppet Press
Holt, Rinehart and Winston
NEW YORK

Library of Congress Cataloging in Publication Data
Gikow, Louise.
The last days of Fraggle Rock.
Summary: The inhabitants of Fraggle Rock rejoice when
the Gorgs leave the Garden for a vacation but soon dis-
cover that the Garden needs care in order to survive.
1. Children's stories, American. [1. Gardens—Fiction.
2. Puppets—Fiction] I. Venning, Sue, ill. II. Title.
PZ7.G369Las 1985 [E] 85-5425
ISBN: 0-03-004548-7

First Edition
Printed in the United States of America
1 3 5 7 9 10 8 6 4 2

ISBN 0-03-004548-7

Contents

Junior Catches a Cold

THE whole thing started the day that Junior Gorg caught a cold.

It was a grayish morning in the Gorgs' Garden, right outside Fraggle Rock. Junior was there, weeding around the tomato plants. And Mokey Fraggle was there, looking for a nice, crisp radish to have for breakfast.

Junior didn't notice Mokey, which was just as well. She was doing the best she could to keep out of his way. Junior doesn't like the Fraggles very much, especially when they pick radishes from his Garden. So Mokey, who has the job of picking radishes for the Fraggles, had become very good at avoiding Junior.

She was sneaking under a Gorgonzalea bush with her chosen radish in her arms, when a big drop of rain fell on her tail. At the same time, another drop plopped on Junior Gorg's nose. A big gray cloud had just reached the Garden, and it was trying to decide if it felt like becoming a good old-fashioned thunder-and-lightning storm.

Hmm, Mokey thought. *It looks like rain. I'd better get back to Fraggle Rock in a hurry.*

"Hmm," said Junior Gorg out loud. "It looks like rain. I'd better finish my chores in a hurry."

Mokey made a dash for the hole in the ground that led to Fraggle Rock. But in her rush to miss the rain, she wasn't as careful as she might have been. Junior had just gotten to the cucumbers, when he looked up and noticed a flashing tail disappearing behind the watermelon patch. "Fwaggle!" he cried, his eyes lighting up. "I'm gonna catch me a Fwaggle!" And he made a flying leap for Mokey—just as the cloud made up its mind and let loose a shower of rain on the Garden.

Mokey reached the hole a Doozer-length ahead of Junior. *Whew!* she thought as she trotted down the tunnel that led to Fraggle Rock. *That was close! At least I didn't get caught— or wet!*

The same could not be said for Junior, however. By the time he gave up on Mokey, put his gardening tools away, and got inside the castle, he was soaked to the skin.

"Junior," Ma said as he stood, dripping on the welcome

mat. "You get out of those clothes this instant, or you're going to catch your death of cold."

"Yes, Ma," said Junior. If you could say nothing else about Junior, you had to admit that he was a very obedient son. He put on dry clothes right away and dried his hair as well as he could. (Since he had hair all over his body, this took quite a bit of doing. He had used seventeen towels by the time he was through!) But he still had a bit of a sniffle that evening at dinner. And by the next morning, he was running a Gorg-size temperature.

"You poor thing," Ma said to Junior. "I'll make you some nice turnip and lima bean soup." Junior was so sick that he only groaned slightly when Ma mentioned the soup. Junior *hates* turnip and lima bean soup.

"Gorg fever," Ma Gorg said to Pa Gorg later, as Junior stared at his soup. "He'll be sick for at least a week."

"The only thing to do is to go someplace to rest and recuperate," Pa replied. "A week or two in the swamp will fix Junior up in a jiffy. Besides, light of my life, you and I haven't been to the swamp in ages."

"But what about the Garden?" Junior sniffled. "Who will take care of my beautiful wadishes?"

"Come on, Junior," said Ma, patting him on his big, hot head. "You wouldn't want the radishes to catch Gorg fever, would you? They'll be just fine. And you can plant a whole new batch when we get home again!"

That was how the whole thing started. What happened next was the most momentous event that had ever occurred in Fraggle Rock!

2

A Strange Occurrence

THE next day, Mokey Fraggle was heading out to pick up her daily quota of radishes when she ran into her roommate, Red. Red was rigging up a new kind of diving board at the edge of the Fraggle Pond. It was made out of bouncebush wood. "When you jump on it," Red explained to the Fraggles who were gathered around, "you'll be able to bounce higher than you ever have before. So a triple toe-loop dive should be as easy as radish pie!"

To show them what she meant, she took the first dive off the new board. *Boing!* went the board, and Red went flying.

"Wow!" she cried. "Bouncy woooooooooood!"

Red flew over the Fraggle Pond, rebounded off a wall, bounced headfirst into Morris Fraggle, and finally fell into the Pond with a huge splash.

"Hey, Mokey!" she cried, coming up for air. "Neat dive, huh?"

"I think you could use just a little less bounce, Red," Mokey said, laughing.

"Where are you headed?" Red asked, pulling herself out of the water and wringing out her tail.

"Over to the Garden," Mokey replied. "Want to come along?"

"Sure!" Red said. "Ouch! Morris sure has a hard head." And the two friends walked off to the Garden together.

It was a beautiful day outside, and the Garden was very green and pleasant. Junior was nowhere to be seen, so the two Fraggles took their time picking out the juiciest radishes and enjoying the sunshine.

"Gee," Red said, pulling hard on a watercress stem. "It sure can be nice out here when the Gorgs aren't around."

"I know," said Mokey, shading her eyes from the sun. "I get inspired to write some of my best poems when I'm in the Garden."

"Why does the Universe need Gorgs anyway?" Red asked, shaking her head. "All they seem to do is bother Fraggles. Wouldn't it be great if they just went away? Then we could get food whenever we wanted to."

"That would be nice," Mokey sighed. "But it will never happen. There have been Gorgs outside of Fraggle Rock as long as there have been Fraggles inside."

"Well, I wish they'd just disappear," grumbled Red.

Mokey remembered Red's words later that afternoon. She was out in the Garden again to pick up a few more radishes when the door to the castle opened. *Oh, no,* she thought. *A Gorg!* She hid under a greaseberry leaf and held her breath.

It was a Gorg, all right. As a matter of fact, it was three Gorgs. And all three of them were carrying big, lumpy bags.

"Good-bye, castle!" Mokey heard Junior say. "And good-bye, Garden. Good-bye, my lovely wadishes. Sleep tight! Junior is going away. But he loves you all." And then, to Mokey's astonishment, the three Gorgs opened the gate and left the Garden!

Mokey could hardly believe her ears or her eyes. She had never seen the Gorgs leave the Garden before. And they had said good-bye! Where were they going? What was happening? She forgot all about gathering radishes and took off for Fraggle Rock as fast as her legs could carry her.

"Red! Gobo! Wembley! Boober!" she cried as she reached the Great Hall. All four of her best friends were there. Red, Gobo, and Wembley were playing Splash'em in the Pond, while Boober sat nearby on a ledge, trying not to get wet. "If I get wet, I'll catch a cold," he explained to

anyone who happened to be near. "It's the third day after the Fraggle Moon, and everyone knows that's a bad day for germs."

He was the first to hear Mokey's shouts. "What's the matter?" he said, jumping down off the ledge. "Are you all right? Is it the end of the world as we know it? Oh, I just knew it was one of those days!"

Gobo, Red, and Wembley stopped their game when they heard the commotion. They climbed out of the Pond and went to Mokey, who was just telling Boober what had happened. "And then they closed the gate and left!" she said breathlessly as her three friends reached her. "Just like that!"

"Just like what?" Gobo asked.

"Yeah. What's up?" Red chimed in.

"The Gorgs!" Mokey's eyes were as round as skipping stones. "I just saw them leave the Garden. With bags and everything! And they said good-bye!"

"The Gorgs said good-bye to you?" Wembley breathed.

"No, silly," said Mokey, "to the radishes."

The five friends looked at one another. Nothing like this had ever happened before.

"Do you think they're coming back?" Wembley asked.

"Of course they are," said Red. "Gorgs have always lived in the Garden."

Gobo shook his head. "I don't know," he said. "No one's *ever* seen the Gorgs leave the Garden. I think we should at least go out and take a look."

"Do we really want to go out there?" Boober asked apprehensively. "It sounds like inviting trouble to me."

"Come on." Gobo headed for the Garden. "We'll just do a little exploring and see what we can find."

So the five Fraggles headed for the Garden to see what was up.

3

The Gorgs Are Gone!

W<small>HEN</small> the Fraggles got to the hole that led out to the Garden, Gobo put his finger to his lips. "Shhh," he whispered. "Just in case the Gorgs came back."

The Fraggles crept quietly out of Fraggle Rock. But Junior was nowhere to be seen. Everything was peaceful and still. There were rows of ripe vegetables and tree creatures singing . . . but there was no sign of Junior or Ma or Pa Gorg.

The Fraggles tiptoed up a row of carrots and down a row of zucchini. They quietly inspected every corner of the Garden. But there were no Gorgs to be found.

"Maybe they're in the castle," Boober whispered after they had stopped for a conference near a large pumpkin.

"Let's take a look, okay?" Red said.

"Oh, no!" Boober was horrified. "It's much too dangerous! We shouldn't go anywhere near there!"

"Don't be silly, Boober," said Red. "We've been in the castle before, and we can take care of ourselves. Come on!"

Red, Gobo, Wembley, and Mokey headed for the castle door. Boober, who was more afraid of staying alone in the Garden than of going with his friends, followed in the rear. "No good will come of this," he muttered, throwing a little dirt over his left shoulder for luck.

Pa had been careful to shut the door behind him when he left, but he had left the window open a tiny bit. Gobo was the first to notice this.

"Hey, Red," he said, "if you give me a boost up to that vine, I can climb up and look inside."

"Okay, Gobo. Just step here." Red linked her two hands together. "Umph," she grunted, hoisting Gobo up until he could reach the vine. The rest was easy. Gobo was up the vine and on the window ledge in no time.

"Well? Well?" Red said impatiently after a few minutes had passed. "What do you see? Any Gorgs around?"

"Doesn't look like it," Gobo called back. "I don't think anybody's home. Come on up and see for yourself!"

"Okay!" Red looked around. "Hey, Mokey. Help me, okay?" And she pointed to a smallish rock that they could use as a step. After she and Mokey had dragged the rock over underneath the window, the two of them climbed up after Gobo. Wembley followed. Boober stayed on the ground, "to warn you if I see trouble coming," he said. "Which I know I will."

Gobo, Red, Wembley, and Mokey peered into the Gorgs' castle. It looked very deserted, and there were big white sheets over all the giant furniture.

Right under the window was a huge table. "Let's take a closer look," Gobo suggested, jumping down.

"I'm with you, Gobo!" Red said. Grabbing a hold of the edge of one of the Gorgs' curtains, she slid down and joined her friend.

"Hey, you two," Wembley gulped, "are you sure this is a good idea?"

"Sure," Gobo said, sounding braver than he really felt. It didn't *look* like there were any Gorgs around, but you never could tell.

"Anyway," Red said, "the Gorgs are so huge that we'll hear them coming a mile away. It'll be fine, Wembley!"

"Well, if you're going in, so am I!" Wembley said. And he jumped down next.

Only Mokey stayed on the window ledge. She was getting almost as nervous as Boober. After all, she was the reason her friends were here. What if she were wrong and the Gorgs were really just in the next room?

Mokey watched as Gobo, Red, and Wembley climbed down the table leg to a chair, and from there to the floor. Then they ran across the floor and disappeared.

She waited and waited, her heart pounding. She was just thinking of going back to Fraggle Rock for help when she saw Red's pigtails appear from behind the leg of a chair.

"Are you all right?" she said fearfully.

"Fine," Gobo replied, poking his head around another leg. "No Gorgs in sight. It sure looks like they're gone."

"Yippee!" cried Red. "This calls for a celebration! No more Gorgs! No more danger! All the radishes we want!"

"It's true, Mokey!" Wembley added. "We went all over the place."

The three of them climbed back up to the window ledge where Mokey stood.

"How long do you think they'll be away?" Wembley asked.

"Forever!" Red cried. "They're never coming back!"

"Well, I'm not so sure about that," Gobo cautioned. "After all, they could be back at any time. We'll still need to keep an eye out for them."

"That should be easy," laughed Red. "Gorgs aren't hard to spot. They're *huge*!"

"Well, let's get back to the Rock," said Gobo as he started to slide down the vine. "After all, no matter how long the Gorgs are gone, this is still pretty exciting news!"

"What is?" asked Boober. Gobo told him. And then the five Fraggles headed back to Fraggle Rock to tell everyone else!

4
A Fraggle Celebration

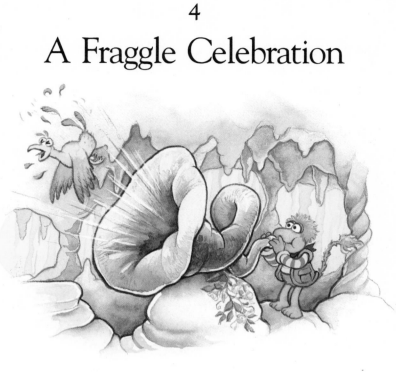

B*LAAH-OOOOG! BLAAH-OOOOG!*

The Fragglehorn sounded up and down the caves and tunnels to Fraggle Rock, summoning thousands of Fraggles to
the Great Hall. The horn was only used on very important
occasions, and as the Fraggles gathered, whispers rippled
throughout the Hall.

"What do you think is the matter?"

"What's up?"

"Who sounded the alarm?"

The last question was soon answered, as Gobo stood up on
a rock in front of the crowd. "Okay! Settle down!" he cried.
"Attention, everyone!"

"What's going on? Why were we called?" Fraggle voices
asked.

"Listen!" He held up his hands. "We have something important to tell you!" He turned to Mokey, who was standing on his right. "You should do it, Mokey," he said. "You were the one who saw the whole thing."

Mokey moved forward, clearing her throat. The Fraggles finally quieted down.

"Everyone," she began, "I have some news. The Gorgs seem to have disappeared! I saw them—"

But her words were drowned out by a roar that came from countless Fraggle throats.

"Disappeared?! The Gorgs have disappeared?! It's a miracle!" The crowd went wild. Fraggles threw their hats in the air. They jumped up and down. They cheered so loudly that twenty-three of them woke up with sore throats the next day.

Gobo held up his hands again. "This calls for a celebration!" he yelled above the noise. "Everybody to the Garden!"

And a thousand Fraggles took off for the tunnel that led out of Fraggle Rock.

Fraggles spilled out into the Garden. They tumbled over one another in their rush to see for themselves that the Gorgs were really gone.

"Hey! This is great!" someone yelled, biting into a radish. "We don't have to drag the radishes back to the Rock. We can eat them right here!" A hundred Fraggle hands dug up fifty of Junior's prize radishes, and countless Fraggle teeth gobbled them up on the spot.

Fraggles danced and sang. They climbed over everything, and under everything, and touched everything. They were free to do whatever they wanted to, and it felt wonderful.

"Anyone want to see where the Gorgs used to live?" Gobo

stood on the window ledge. "Come one, come all!" he cried, pointing to the castle. "See the original home of the giant Gorgs, fearsome keepers of the Garden! It's thrilling! It's chilling! It's *big*!"

Before long, Fraggles were crawling inside the Gorgs' castle. The Gorgs were gone! Junior would never catch another Fraggle again. Things couldn't be better!

But somewhere in the Garden, hidden behind a rutabaga, a small green shoot pushed its way out of the ground. Another emerged next to a young carrot. The Fraggles didn't know it, but they were about to meet up with a problem that was a lot bigger than Junior Gorg.

5

Trouble in the Garden

For the next few days, the Fraggles had a wonderful time
out in the Garden. Red organized some relay races, and
Boober discovered that Fraggles can get sunburned. Gobo
explored to his heart's content, and Wembley joined everyone and did everything.

As the discoverer of the Great Gorg Migration, as it came
to be known, Mokey was cheered all over Fraggle Rock. She
spent her days sitting in a quiet corner of the Garden, recit-
ing her poems to a circle of admiring young Fraggles. Her job
was still to gather the radishes, of course; but since all the

Fraggles could now go eat outside, there wasn't much for her to do.

Three days after the great celebration, Mokey woke up feeling as hungry as a Doozer construction team. Grabbing a few Doozer sticks on the way, she headed to the Garden for breakfast.

A nice radish, she thought as she trotted happily along. *That'll be just the thing.* And she sang the first verse of a special Garden song she had started to write the day before:

> "The Gorgs have gone away. Hurray!
> The Fraggles all will play today!
> Our world is safe and free, whoopee!
> Ta-da, ta-da, ta-dee. Ta-dee!"

By the time she got to the second "ta-dee," she had reached the Garden.

It was still very early, and Mokey was the first one there. She stretched her arms up to the warm sun and said a quiet thank you to Nature for such a lovely day. Then she headed over to the radish patch for her morning meal.

She had walked almost to the castle walls before she realized that she had somehow passed the radishes. *That's odd,* she thought. *I didn't even see them! I must still be pretty sleepy.* She rubbed her eyes, turned around, and walked back, stopping where she knew the radishes would be.

But there were no radishes there.

Mokey was a little confused. *I'm sure they were here yesterday,* she thought, frowning. *Or maybe it was the day before. I remember picking a lot of them.* There had been a big radish bake-off and Fraggles had cooked up all sorts of wonderful radish dishes. Boober won, of course—his radish-and-carrot roast with spinach stuffing always took first prize.

But now, all Mokey could see were green leaves and twisting vines. They didn't look anything like radishes . . . *and they don't taste anything like radishes, either!* she thought, biting into one of the strange-looking plants. *Yuck! Bitter!*

Well, I'll try some peas, she thought next, walking over to the next row of plants. The strange green vines were here, too, but at least she saw a few pea pods. But instead of fat, juicy green peas, she found tiny, shriveled-up brownish-green lumps!

Something is definitely wrong here, Mokey thought. *I'd better go get some help.* And she headed back to Fraggle Rock.

What Mokey didn't know was that Junior's absence was taking its toll on the Garden. Junior had always planted and weeded and watered the vegetables. Since he hadn't done his chores for a while, the Garden had begun to get dry and overgrown. Plants were dying of thirst, and the bitter green vines that Mokey had tasted were weeds. Weeds were choking the artichokes and strangling the string beans. They were quickly taking over every patch of ground in sight.

But the Fraggles didn't know very much about gardening—they thought that radishes and parsnips and celery just grew. If anyone had tried to tell them that Junior took care of the vegetables and actually provided the Fraggles with their food, they wouldn't have believed a word of it.

And in fact, when Mokey told Gobo that something was the matter with the Garden, he didn't believe a word of it either.

"Aw, come on, Mokey," he said. "Nothing is ever wrong with the Garden. You're probably just imagining things. Maybe you went to the wrong place or something."

"Gobo Fraggle!" Mokey cried indignantly. "I've been gathering radishes as long as . . . as long as . . . you've been an explorer! I should know where they're supposed to be. They're gone! Come out and see for yourself!"

"Okay. But I'm sure there's some simple explanation." And Gobo let Mokey lead him into the Garden.

"You see?!" she said, pointing at the huge mess of weeds that was Junior's radish patch. "Do you see any radishes? All

there is are those strange plants. And a lot of the other vegetables are all dried out. Gobo, we have to face it—there is hardly any food left up here!"

"This can't be happening," Gobo muttered. And he started to walk up and down the Garden in search of vegetables. But each row told the same sad story. A lack of water and the strangling weeds had quickly turned the Garden into a wasteland.

Gobo rejoined Mokey again at the former home of the radishes. She was sitting on the ground, looking helplessly into the tangle of weeds.

"Don't worry, Mokey." Gobo put his hand on her shoulder. "We'll figure out something. In the meantime, we'll just have to live on Doozer sticks."

Mokey got to her feet, and the two of them slowly walked back to Fraggle Rock.

6

Is This the End?

A few days later, Gobo, Mokey, Red, Wembley, and Boober sat in the Great Hall. It was time for lunch and they were very hungry. But no one bothered to go out to the Garden. There was nothing there to eat.

And that wasn't the only problem. Besides there being no more food in the Garden, no Doozer constructions were being built either. In fact, Fraggle Rock had been suspiciously empty of Doozers all morning.

"Boy, I'm starved," said Gobo, sighing. "I keep thinking about a nice, steaming-hot piece of radish loaf with squash sauce, just the way Boober makes it."

"Don't remind me," said Red. "Everything is beginning to look like a radish to me. When I close my eyes, all I see are big, red, juicy . . ."

"Stop!" Wembley moaned, holding his stomach.

"I wonder where the Doozers are." Mokey sighed. "A Doozer stick would be really tasty right about now."

"Or two or three," Wembley added.

"The Doozers won't come," Boober said. "This is obviously a disaster of Global Proportions. There will never be anything to eat here in Fraggle Rock again. We will be forced to leave our homeland and venture out into the wilderness, our belongings on our backs, homeless and hungry and—"

"Would you quit it?" Gobo snapped.

"Well!" Boober sniffed. "I'm only stating the obvious. If you want to yell at me . . ."

"Don't mind Gobo," Mokey said softly. "He's hungry. It makes everyone snappish."

"But the truth is," Red said slowly, "that we will have to leave Fraggle Rock if something doesn't happen fast."

The five friends looked at one another. "Leave Fraggle Rock," Wembley said wonderingly. "Where would we go? We've always lived in Fraggle Rock."

"I don't know." Gobo frowned. "I was looking at Uncle Traveling Matt's maps this morning. As far as we know, there are other communities of Fraggles, but I'm not sure where they are, and I don't know what they eat. We might try to find them. Or we could travel into Outer Space . . . Uncle Matt seems to eat well enough there."

"Go into Outer Space?" Boober's eyes were wide with fear. "There's no way *I'm* going into Outer Space. It's dangerous out there! There's the Beast, and the Silly Creatures, and all sorts of terrible things! I'm not going anywhere *near* Outer Space!"

"Don't worry, Boober," Mokey said. "It's not time to move yet. There has to be something we can do."

"What do you suppose happened to the Garden?" Wembley asked.

"Maybe the Gorgs poisoned it before they left," Boober suggested.

"That's just the kind of nasty thing a Gorg would do," Red nodded. "They've always been mean to Fraggles."

"Or maybe something big and terrible has moved into the castle and is eating everything up!" Boober began to get very excited.

"Big and terrible and invisible," Gobo pointed out. "If anything had moved into the castle lately, we would have noticed."

"Or it could be vegetable germs," Boober suggested. "Or a radish plague. Or . . ."

"Enough, Boober." Gobo frowned. "Whatever caused it isn't really that important. The point is . . . is there anything we can do about it?"

"Gobo, you were talking about Outer Space before," Mokey said. "When you go out there to get the postcards from your Uncle Traveling Matt, have you ever seen any radishes?"

"No," Gobo sighed, shaking his head. "Besides the postcards, I usually only pay attention to the Beast. But I'm sure I would have noticed if radishes were growing there."

"There's got to be *something* we can do!" Red stamped her foot impatiently.

"At least if the Doozers were making Doozer sticks, we could live on them until we figured it all out," Gobo said.

"But Doozer-stick production seems to have stopped, too."

"Yeah. Go figure it," Red said. "Just when we need them the most, the little guys disappear!"

"Wait a minute." Mokey's eyes grew bright. "Why don't we send a . . . a . . . Fraggle delegation to the Doozers? We could ask them to start building again. Work out some sort of compromise for the good of the Rock. A system of peaceful cooperation, in harmony with the balance of nature . . ."

"Don't get carried away, Mokey." Red patted her roommate on the arm.

"You know, I think Mokey has a point," Gobo said, staring into space. "Maybe we should try talking to the Doozers."

"Well, then, I nominate Mokey to head the delegation!" Red cried. "She's the most diplomatic of all of us."

"And I nominate Gobo to go along," said Wembley.

Gobo and Mokey looked at each other. "Well," Gobo said finally, "if we're going to do this, we might as well get started."

And the two of them headed for the place that the Doozers called home—with the fate of Fraggle Rock resting on their shoulders.

7
The Great Fraggle Migration

G<small>OBO</small> and Mokey were almost at the Doozerdome when they saw a small party of Doozers approaching them.

"Maybe they're coming to talk to us!" Mokey whispered.

"I don't think so," Gobo murmured back. "Doozers never talk to Fraggles."

Indeed, Doozers generally ignore Fraggles whenever they come across them. And even though it is hard to ignore a Fraggle who is standing directly in your path, the Doozers politely tried to pretend that Mokey and Gobo weren't really there at all.

"We can bring the children through here," said one of the Doozers.

"All right," said a second. "But we'll have to drag the heavy machinery through the west tunnel. It's the only one that's big enough."

Gobo and Mokey stood there for a while, waiting for something to happen. The Doozers kept on pretending that the Fraggles weren't there. Finally, Gobo cleared his throat.

"Uh . . . excuse me, Doozers," he said. "Uh, Doozers? Stop!"

"What are those silly Fraggles doing standing there?" one of the Doozers said. "Can't they see we're busy?"

"Fraggles never care if you're busy," said another. "They don't know the meaning of the word *work*."

"Uh, Doozer?" Mokey took over. "There's something we need to talk to you about."

"Talk to us?" a Doozer replied. "Fraggles never talk to us."

"We do now," said Gobo. "We need to discuss something. Why aren't you building any more constructions? And what are you doing?"

"These Fraggles are crazy," said the first Doozer, politely looking down at his shoes. "We're the reconnaissance team. We're moving. Going away. The mines are empty. Of course there are no more constructions. There is no more radish dust. We must find a place where we can build once again. Without work, there is no life."

"Radish dust?" Mokey said, confused. "What are you talking about?"

The Doozers shook their heads.

"Silly Fraggles." And then they walked past Mokey and Gobo and disappeared down the tunnel.

The two Fraggles stood there helplessly. They had no idea that Doozers actually dug tunnels under the Gorgs' Garden and mined the radishes and vegetables and made Doozer sticks out of them. The Doozer radish mines had died when the Garden died. That's why the Doozers had stopped building and why they were moving.

"Maybe Boober was right," Mokey finally said. "This is a disaster of Global Proportions. It can't just be a coincidence that the Doozers are leaving Fraggle Rock just when we're faced with famine, can it?"

"I don't know," Gobo sighed. "I don't understand any of it. But we'd better go back to the Great Hall. It looks like we may have to be moving, too."

Gobo stood on a high rock in the Great Hall, which overlooked a huge crowd of Fraggles. He and Mokey had sounded the Fragglehorn when they returned from talking to the Doozers.

"So it looks like the Doozers are leaving Fraggle Rock, too," Gobo was saying. "Mokey and I don't see any choice. We're going to have to move to find food."

"It can't be!" Fraggles cried. "Leave our homes? It's horrible!"

They looked at one another helplessly. But there seemed to be no other solution. They would have to leave Fraggle Rock.

"I'd better gather my maps," Gobo said quietly. "We'll need them."

"And we all have to pack," Mokey added. "Come on, Red."

One by one the Fraggles slowly left the Great Hall. The Great Fraggle Migration was about to begin.

8
Welcome Home

MOKEY was better at packing than Red, so she was ready to go long before her roommate. She sat and watched as Red threw things around.

"My Tug-o-Tails trophy," Red muttered to herself. "Got to take that. And my thwacka ball. And what would I do without *this*?" Red held up something sort of lumpy that Mokey didn't recognize.

"What *is* that, Red?" she asked.

"I'm not sure," Red answered. "But I've always had it. I can't just leave it behind!"

Mokey shook her head, smiling slightly. Then she got up and walked to the door.

"I'm going to go out to the Garden one more time," she said quietly. "To say good-bye."

"I'll go with you," Red offered.

"If you don't mind . . ." Mokey hesitated. "I'd rather be alone, Red. Is that okay?"

"I understand." Red put her arms around Mokey and hugged her hard. "I'll be here waiting for you."

Mokey walked down paths she had always walked down and through tunnels that knew her step. As she passed each familiar rock, she touched it and whispered a small farewell. Her heart was heavy with grief. Leaving Fraggle Rock was the hardest thing any Fraggle had ever done.

She finally reached the hole to the Garden. It was a beautiful day, bright and sunny. But what was that strange noise? It sounded like a thousand bumblebees buzzing.

"Dum de dum, hmmmmmm," went the noise. "Boy, this Garden sure needs a lot of work. I'm sorry, wadishes, for leaving you. But I'll have you fat and happy again in no time!"

Mokey couldn't believe her ears. She lifted up her head to take a look. It was Junior! He was back, busily working in the Garden. And the Garden! Mokey held her breath and closed her eyes. Then she opened them again. All the nasty green plants were gone. And the tiny tips of baby vegetables were sticking out of the soil!

Mokey's mouth was open in astonishment. She crawled out of the hole and just stood there. What was going on? Could the Gorg have come back to take care of the Garden?

The thought was so amazing to Mokey that she held her breath. The Gorg take care of the Garden! Didn't that mean, in some sort of way, that the Gorg took care of the Fraggles? After all, the Fraggles got most of their food from the Garden. And if the Gorg kept the Garden growing . . . Mokey was so stunned by this possibility that she didn't even notice that Junior Gorg had seen her.

"A Fwaggle!" he whispered happily to himself. "Oh, how I've missed chasing Fwaggles! Come here, Fwaggle!" And he tiptoed toward Mokey.

Luckily, a Gorg trying to tiptoe is like a volcano trying to erupt without waking the neighbors. Mokey noticed Junior when he was still a few feet away. She made it back into Fraggle Rock before you could say "Oh, radishes!"—which is what Junior said when she disappeared. But there was a lot of work to be done in the Garden, and Junior soon forgot about Mokey and went back to his weeding and planting and watering.

Mokey ran all the way back to Fraggle Rock. "They're back! They're back!" she cried as she ran. "Everyone, they're back! They're back!"

A group of Fraggles, including Gobo and Wembley, were gathered in the Great Hall when Mokey burst in. "They're back!" she shouted. "They're back!"

"Who's back, Mokey?" asked Gobo.

"The radishes! And the Gorgs! Everything is back! Isn't it

wonderful? And Gobo, there's something I understood when I was out in the Garden. We *need* the Gorgs!"

"Mokey, are you feeling alright?" Wembley asked, looking concerned. "You sound very strange."

"You don't understand!" Mokey cried. "It's all in the balance of nature! Oh, just come *on!*" And Mokey took Gobo by one hand and Wembley by the other. "We're going to the Garden!"

Fraggle Rock is known for its celebrations. Often, when Fraggles remember happy times, they will say, "There's never been a party quite like the one we gave for Milton Fraggle when he beat the all-time Cave Jumping record!" or, "We've never thrown a better party than we did for Boober and Red when they were rescued from that cave-in down by the Spiral Cavern." But there never, ever, *ever* was a party like the one they threw in Fraggle Rock to celebrate the Return of the Vegetables. There wasn't a whole lot of food—the radishes weren't full-grown yet, and Mokey didn't want to pick too many of them. But there was more than enough happiness to go around, and the Fraggles feasted on that.

In a few days, the Garden grew some more, and Doozer-stick production began again. But it was a long time before the Fraggles stopped talking about the time they almost had to leave Fraggle Rock.

"I wish we could understand what happened," said Wembley to Gobo one day, as they swished their toes in the Fraggle Pond. "Everything in Fraggle Rock just seemed to go away. First the Gorgs, and then the vegetables, and then the

Doozers . . . I guess it was all a part of some mysterious Natural Event."

"Whatever it was, everything came back again," said Gobo cheerfully. "Although it's too bad that the Gorgs had to come back, too."

"What do you suppose Mokey was talking about when she said we needed the Gorgs?" Wembley asked.

Gobo shrugged. "I'm not sure. She was under a lot of strain. But we'll figure the whole thing out someday. And by the way—speaking of radishes, do you want to go up to the Garden for a snack?"

Gobo smiled at Wembley, and Wembley smiled back. And even though the Fraggles never knew that the Gorgs left the Garden because Junior got a bad cold, and the vegetables

died because Junior wasn't there to take care of them, and the Doozers stopped building because Doozer sticks are made out of radishes—well, even though the Fraggles never really understood all of those things, the story still has a happy ending. And this is it!